Our Family Is Divorcing

A Read-Aloud Book
for Families Experiencing Divorce

Patricia Polin Johnson • *Donna Reilly Williams*

Illustrated by Bud Vogt

Resource Publications, Inc.
San Jose, California

Editorial director: Kenneth Guentert
Prepress manager: Elizabeth J. Asborno
Copyeditor: Leila T. Bulling

Reprint Department
Resource Publications, Inc.
160 E. Virginia Street #290
San Jose, CA 95112-5876
408-286-8505 (voice)
408-287-8748 (fax)

Library of Congress Cataloging-in-Publication Data
Johnson, Patricia Polin, 1958-
    Our family is divorcing : a read-aloud book for families experiencing divorce /
Patricia Polin Johnson, Donna Reilly Williams.
        p.   cm. — (Helping children who hurt)
    Summary: Mandy and her two brothers are distressed when their parents decide
that they cannot live together anymore and announce that they are getting a
divorce.
    ISBN 0-89390-391-4 (pbk.)
    [1. Divorce—Fiction.] I. Williams, Donna Reilly, 1945-   . II. Title. III. Series.
PZ7.J635350u   1996
[E]—dc20   96-26335

Printed in the United States of America

00 99 98 97 96 I 5 4 3 2 1

Also available from the
HELPING CHILDREN WHO HURT
Series

Morgan's Baby Sister

Series edited by Donna Reilly Williams

To my parents, Ray and Rose Polin, and to A. J. and Matthew, who all taught me how to love.
— P. P. J.

To Benjamin, Kameron, and Carter.
May you find love and security in your lives.
— D. R. W.

Contents

1 *Our Family Is Divorcing*

64 To the Caregiver

69 Notes about *Our Family Is Divorcing*

74 Questions for Discussion

Our Family Is Divorcing

"Whatcha got there, Mandy Pants?" Mandy's younger brother, Spencer, peeked into her bedroom.

"Don't call me that." Mandy stuck out her tongue. "If you must know, it's a scrapbook from our trip. Go get Eddie, and I'll let you both look at it."

Spencer ran to find four-year-old Eddie, and moments later, they both burst into the room and plopped onto the bed with her.

Carefully, Mandy opened her album to the first page. Eddie reached to touch it, and she quickly pushed his hand away.

"Don't touch!" she said. "I'll turn the pages. This is a picture of the beach house, remember?" Mandy could almost smell the sea breeze again and feel the warm sunshine on her back.

"What's this, Mandy?" Eddie pointed to some dried flowers glued to the page.

"Daddy helped me pick those at the point of the cape," she said. "We found a beautiful wild garden that he named 'Mandy's Meadow.'"

"And here's Mommy and me and the bucket of shells we collected," Eddie said with excitement.

"Don't crowd!" Mandy warned. How she longed for a sister! Why was she stuck with two brothers?

"Ouch, Mandy! Spencer, get off of my hand!" shouted the smallest brother.

"You kids stop all that noise!" Mommy's voice rose from downstairs.

"Now see what you've done," Mandy scolded. "Just let me turn the pages."

"Look at this!" Spencer said. "Barney with my slipper in his mouth." Barney, their Golden Retriever, had lived with them for as long as the children could remember, and he always vacationed with the family while Mrs. Twitmeyer, their parakeet, and Priscilla, the cat, stayed home with the next-door neighbors.

"I don't remember this one," Spencer said, pointing to a picture of Mommy and Daddy sitting on the cottage porch.

Mandy remembered all too well. Sneaking up to take a surprise picture, she had heard Mommy and Daddy arguing, again.

"You're never home," Mommy had said.

"But that's my job," answered Daddy. "I have to provide for you and the kids, don't I?"

They had turned abruptly when Mandy interrupted them. "Smile," she had said, pressing the button on the camera. Now, seeing the picture of Mommy smiling with tears in her eyes made Mandy's stomach hurt, and her heart raced just as it had that day.

Mandy leaned back against her pillows while Spencer and Eddie continued to fight over the scrapbook. Even though they had been home from vacation for just over a month, it seemed like a million years ago. Ever since they had come back, Mandy had noticed changes around the house.

For one thing, Daddy was sleeping in the guest room now. Mommy and Daddy had told Mandy that it was because Daddy had a cold and didn't want to disturb Mommy's sleep. But Mandy hadn't seen him sniffle or cough in the longest time. Why didn't he go back to their bedroom, Mandy wondered. And yesterday, why had she seen Daddy moving his toothbrush and razor to the guest bathroom?

4

Mandy had asked Mommy about that, but Mommy hadn't really explained the reason and had asked Mandy not to tell the boys because they might worry. Mandy didn't understand that, but she hadn't told them. Now, she tried to make herself think about something else.

They heard Daddy's voice from downstairs. "Mandy, Spencer, Eddie! I'm off now." He was leaving on another business trip.

Mandy and Eddie raced each other down the stairs. Spencer followed quietly.

Daddy hugged them and tickled Eddie under the chin. "You be good now, okay? And I'll be back when the bees squeeze their knees." None of them, including Daddy, knew what that phrase meant, but he said it every time he went away. They loved it, and it had become a family tradition.

Mandy didn't like that Daddy traveled so much for his job, but she felt she had to be brave for her brothers. Besides, Daddy always called every night when he was away, and he sent them postcards from wherever he went. He also brought them each a little gift when he came home. Mandy appreciated Daddy's efforts to make his time away from them as painless as possible.

"Farewell, Mandy Bug," Daddy said. He picked her up, and she snuggled against his neck. She loved the way her daddy smelled.

"I'll say extra prayers for you, Daddy," she said.

"Thanks, Honey. I'll say extra prayers for you, too. Eddie, take care of the family while I'm gone." He stooped to pick up the little boy, but Eddie reached to shake Daddy's hand.

"Barney and I will protect everyone, Dad," Eddie said. He had announced several times before that he wanted to be just like Daddy when he grew up.

Six-year-old Spencer had watched them from the corner of the hallway. Mandy knew *he* hated to see Daddy go. He always cried when Daddy closed the door.

"See you, Sport," Daddy said to Spencer. "Don't forget I promised to help you fix your bike when I get back. I'm going to keep that promise, just you wait."

Spencer liked to help Daddy with jobs like working in the garage and raking leaves.

"When the bees squeeze their knees, right, Daddy?" he said, in a small voice.

"You bet," Daddy said. "I love you, Son."

"You'd better leave, or you'll miss your plane." Mommy's voice sounded cranky and impatient and angry, all at the same time.

"Right," Daddy said. "I'll call when I get there."

"Fine," answered Mommy.

"Fine," Daddy said, like an echo. Then he walked out the door and closed it behind him.

Time usually passed quickly for Mandy even when Daddy was gone. She enjoyed her school and found that the third grade was quite easy. She loved to read, was an excellent speller, and usually finished her arithmetic problems before anyone in the class. Mommy, Daddy, and Mr. Esquivel, her favorite teacher so far, often told her how proud they were of her. The school was only two blocks from home, and everyone there was friendly and kind.

She liked her after-school activities, too. On Monday, she went to Scouts, on Tuesday, she had violin lessons, and on Wednesday, she had swimming lessons. On Thursday, they all went to the library with Mommy, and on Friday, Barbara and Rose came over to play. Before she knew it, it was time for Daddy to come home.

"He's here!" Spencer shouted on Friday night. He had been watching for Daddy for at least an hour. He flung open the door just as Daddy was pulling out his keys.

"Hey, Sport," Daddy said. "Have the bees squeezed their knees?"

Spencer hugged Daddy with all his strength. Mandy and Eddie ran to the door, greeting Daddy with laughter and hugs. Mommy stayed in the kitchen and stirred the soup.

For some reason Mandy couldn't sleep that night, so she walked downstairs for a glass of milk. The light was on in the kitchen. Mandy stopped at the dining room when she heard Mommy and Daddy arguing.

"You don't care about me anymore," she heard Mommy say. Mandy could tell Mommy was crying. Did Daddy make her cry? she wondered. Why would Daddy do that?

"You don't respect me, either," Daddy said. "I work every day to provide for you and the kids."

"You aren't home enough to provide the things they really need, like love and discipline." Mommy's voice quivered.

"Maybe we should do something about that, permanently." Daddy's voice sounded stern and sad.

Mandy's stomach churned, and her heart raced. She turned around and tiptoed back to bed.

"Please, God," she prayed. "Please help Mommy and Daddy stop fighting so much. I promise I'll be extra nice to Spencer and Eddie if you make them stop."

She heard Mommy and Daddy coming up the stairs. She closed her eyes when Mommy peeked into her room. Then she heard Mommy and Daddy each close the doors to their separate bedrooms.

The next morning, Mandy overslept. She dressed quickly and ran downstairs. Looking out the front window, she could see Spencer and Daddy raking and bagging leaves. In the kitchen, Eddie was finishing his juice, and Mommy was washing dishes.

"I have some warm waffles for you in the oven," Mommy said to Mandy. Mommy served Mandy's breakfast and then went outside.

Mandy chewed each bite slowly and used the last bite to soak up the syrup on her plate. Just as she swallowed it, Mommy, Daddy, and Spencer came into the kitchen.

"Children," Mommy said, "your father and I have something to tell you." She and Daddy both looked sad.

Daddy sat on the chair next to Mandy, and Mommy picked up Eddie and held him on her lap. Spencer climbed onto Daddy's lap. Everyone was very quiet. Mandy knew something important was about to happen.

"There are going to be some changes in our family," Daddy said slowly, looking at the floor. "Mommy and I have decided that we cannot live together anymore. This is no one's fault," he said, looking up, "certainly not you children's fault. But Mommy and I have become different people, and the differences are too great for us to live together."

"We are very unhappy about the way things are right now," Mommy continued. "Daddy and I tried our best to get along with each other, but it isn't working. We still love you very much. That will never change."

"You'll always be our children," Daddy said. "And we will always be your Mommy and Daddy. But we have decided to get a divorce. That means Mommy and I don't want to be married to each other anymore."

"But we're not divorcing you," Mommy said quickly. "We're divorcing each other."

"Things will be mixed up for a while," Daddy said. "But for now, you'll all live here with Mommy, and next weekend, I will go to live someplace else. After I'm settled in a new house, you can come to visit me."

No one said a word. Only Barney's tail banging against the cupboard door broke the silence. Eddie, in Mommy's lap, sucked his thumb as Mommy gently rocked him. Mandy saw a tear roll down Mommy's cheek.

Spencer suddenly burst into tears and buried his face in Daddy's chest. Then Mandy saw something she had never seen before. She saw Daddy cry. Really cry.

Mandy wanted to say, "No, Daddy. Mommy, don't do this!" But she just couldn't get her voice to speak. She felt scared. All she could do was stare down at her plate and watch her big teardrops mix with maple syrup.

That week, Mommy and Daddy seemed extra nice to Mandy and the boys. Mandy thought *maybe* they had changed their minds about the divorce. She decided not to say anything to remind them about it, just in case.

But they hadn't changed their minds.

Mommy woke the children early on Sunday and asked everyone to dress neatly.

"I want to take you to the harvest festival after church, and then we're going to the movies," she said.

"What about Daddy?" Spencer asked.

"Daddy has some things to put together today," Mommy answered.

Spencer and Eddie usually fidgeted during church, but today they sat quietly next to Mommy.

"Please, God," Mandy prayed. "Please make everything okay at our house."

At the harvest festival, Mommy bought Mandy a wooden scarecrow with a pumpkin head and some wooden puzzles for the boys. Mandy noticed all the other mommies and daddies together with their children.

After the festival, they went to a movie about some animals trying to find their way home. But Mandy couldn't pay attention.

"Do you think Daddy needs my help at home? "she whispered to Mommy.

"No, Dear," Mommy whispered back. "I'm sure he's doing everything he needs to do."

The sun was beginning to go down when they arrived home. Daddy's car was still in the driveway. Maybe he was staying! But when Mandy opened the front door, she found Daddy's suitcases nearby.

Daddy was in the den putting some papers into his briefcase. He snapped it shut and came out to the hall.

Mommy closed the front door, glanced at Daddy, and then went upstairs.

The children gathered around Daddy, and they all walked slowly into the family room and toward the fireplace. Running his hand along the mantle, he smiled faintly when his fingers touched the nails where they hung their Christmas stockings each year.

He turned around and walked back to the den. The children stood by the hall door and watched him, without saying anything. He looked at his desk and the bookshelves. His shoulders slumped as he picked up a wooden cross he had brought from Spain. Mandy loved to touch the smooth cool wood, and she always thought she could still smell the live tree it had come from.

Walking back to the children, Daddy took Mandy's hand and led her into the family room. He knelt beside her and handed her the cross. "Take care of this, Mandy Bug," he said. "Think about me whenever you pick it up, and remember how much I love you."

"Okay, Daddy," she said, feeling tears trickle down her cheeks and across her nose.

Daddy walked out of the den and toward the front door.

"Give me a hug," he said, turning toward the children. They grabbed onto his legs. They were all crying now.

"Till the bees squeeze..." Daddy said, and he stopped.

"Their knees," choked Mandy.

Daddy opened the door, and after hugging the children once more, he picked up his two big suitcases and walked out. The children watched from the porch as he put his suitcases into the car and backed down the driveway.

They waved and waved and waved at him as he drove down the street. Then he turned the corner and was gone from sight.

Mandy shivered and realized that the sun had set and night had begun.

The next morning, Mandy slept in and was almost late to school. She couldn't concentrate on her spelling test or the arithmetic problems Mr. Esquivel did on the board. She thought of only one thing: Daddy left home.

She just had to tell somebody. At recess, she called Barbara and Rose over.

"I have an awful secret," she said. "Don't tell anyone what I'm going to tell you. Promise!" They promised.

"My parents are getting a divorce," Mandy whispered. "Daddy left yesterday, to live someplace else."

"That's awful!" Barbara and Rose said in unison.

"What did you do to make him go away?" Barbara asked.

"I didn't do anything!" Mandy answered.

"Emily Wilson's parents got a divorce because she fought so much with her little sister," Barbara said. "Emily told me so."

Mandy didn't think that was the reason Daddy left, but she wasn't too sure.

Mommy seemed happy that week. She didn't scold Eddie when he spilled his grape juice on the carpet. Mandy heard her tell Mrs. O'Connor, Mommy's friend, that she felt "relieved."

Mommy let Mandy and the boys stay up an hour past their bedtime all week; she even let them have ice cream for dinner one night. Just ice cream! Mommy seemed to like the change in their house. Mandy had to admit that it was quiet.

That night, Mandy talked to God about the changes.

"God, I don't know why you let this happen," she said, blinking back tears. "We need our Daddy here. Mommy needs him, too, even if she doesn't act like it. Please bring Daddy home. I promise to be nicer to Spencer and Eddie. I promise to stop fighting with them."

"Mandy, are you awake?" Spencer tapped Mandy's shoulder just as she was drifting off to sleep. "Mandy!"

"What's the matter?" she asked.

"Who's going to help me fix my bike now? Mommy can't do it. She doesn't know how. Why did Daddy go away? Do you think he's ever coming back? Do you think he'll ever forgive Mommy and want to be married to her again?" Spencer's voice was thin and high, and Mandy saw a tear shine on his cheek.

"I don't know, Spencer," she answered in a whisper. "I'm sure Daddy will still help you fix your bike. And I'm sure Mommy didn't *make* Daddy go away. They just couldn't live together, that's all. It's no one's fault."

Mandy wasn't as sure as she tried to sound. She tried to repeat the words as Mommy and Daddy had said them that awful morning last week. Just then, Eddie walked into the room.

"I know why Daddy's leaving," Eddie said. "He's leaving because of me, because I was so bad." The little boy's chin quivered as he spoke.

"No, he isn't, Eddie," Mandy said, putting her arms around him. "Daddy and Mommy are divorcing because they can't get along anymore. We can help by trying to be nicer to each other, and we can pray that they want to stay married."

The three of them got down on their knees beside Mandy's bed.

"Make Daddy stay here with us," Mandy prayed.

"Don't let Daddy forget us," Spencer prayed.

"Make me a better boy," Eddie prayed.

"Amen," they all said.

"Can I get in bed with you?" asked Spencer. "I don't want to sleep alone."

"Me, too," Eddie said.

"Climb in," answered Mandy. She was glad for the company.

While the boys fell right asleep, Mandy lay awake, staring at the ceiling. Her tears began to fall again.

"God, take care of Daddy," she prayed. "I already miss him so much." Mandy squeezed her eyes with concentration. "And please, God, make him call us tomorrow."

For Mandy, the days after that seemed to drag. She didn't like school anymore. She didn't want to go to her after-school activities or play with her friends. She felt tired all the time.

Mommy seemed to be changing, too. She cut her hair and started dressing differently. She seemed happier.

Mandy came home from school a couple of weeks later and heard Mommy talking on the phone.

"Well, finally," she was saying. "These poor kids have been waiting to see you. They've been driving me crazy with questions about where you are and when you'll call."

"Is that Daddy?" asked Mandy. Mommy handed her the phone.

"Daddy?" she said hopefully.

"Hello, Mandy Bug," Daddy answered. "I've got great news. I have a new house. Now you and the boys can come visit me."

Mandy wasn't sure this was such good news. It meant that Daddy wasn't coming home.

"It's just the right house for us," Daddy continued. "It's not far from Mommy's house. In fact, I was hoping to pick up you and the boys in a few minutes, so I can show it to you."

"Is that okay with Mommy?" asked Mandy.

"Let me talk with her again, okay? I'll see you very soon."

Mandy handed the phone to Mommy and listened to her talk.

"Well, it's not very convenient now. I have to help Mandy with her homework....They're next door playing with Ted and Vinny....Okay, okay. But you'll have to pick them up yourself." Then she hung up the phone.

"Go get the boys from next door," she told Mandy. "Your father said he'll be here in fifteen minutes. But I bet it'll be closer to an hour."

Mandy wished Mommy wouldn't say mean things about Daddy. He said he'd come, and Mandy knew he'd keep his word.

Mommy fixed them a quick dinner of macaroni and cheese. They seemed to eat a lot of that lately. Tonight, Mommy cut up some hot dogs in the macaroni. Even though this was Spencer's favorite dinner, he didn't feel much like eating. He kept running to the front window to watch for Daddy. A long time had gone by, and Mandy knew from the clock on the kitchen wall that it had been forty-five minutes.

"He's here!" shouted Spencer. The children ran to the front door to greet Daddy. They stopped abruptly at the door and stared at him.

"How do you like my beard?" Daddy asked. Mandy wasn't sure. This didn't look like the Daddy who had gone away a couple of weeks ago, but he sounded the same. She went closer, and he reached out and hugged her. Snuggling into Daddy's chest, she felt the rough wool of his jacket and smelled his familiar Daddy smell.

All the children were hugging Daddy now, and he stood up with Eddie still clinging to his neck.

"Mandy, tell your mother we're leaving," he said. "I'll meet you in the car."

Daddy's new house needed some paint, and it wasn't very big. The kitchen had blue and white squares on the floor. Through the window, Mandy could see a small patio and a grassy yard surrounded by a high fence.

"Let me show you upstairs," said Daddy. "I have a wonderful surprise for you." They all followed Daddy, who bounded up the stairs two at a time.

"This is your bedroom, Mandy. And over there is Eddie's. And Spencer, this one is yours." Daddy was running from room to room, and the children just watched him from the hallway.

"You mean, I have my own room?" asked Spencer. "I don't have to share with Eddie?"

"That's right," said Daddy. "Your very own room."

Eddie looked at his room and then at the other rooms.

"My room is too far away from everyone else," he said. "I might not like it here."

"I *know* you'll like it, Son," said Daddy in a gentle voice. "It'll just take some getting used to. It's always hard to make changes."

Mandy walked into her new room. It wasn't very big. An old yellow sheet hung across the window.

She hadn't thought about this before. She already had a room at their old house. Which room would be her *real* room? Where would she keep her clothes? Where would she get a bed for this room? In which room would she mark how much she had grown?

She knew Daddy was watching her from the doorway, but she didn't know what to say.

Spencer ran up to them. "Where is your room, Daddy?" he asked.

"Oh, I'll sleep on the couch in the living room," he said.

"You can share my room," Eddie said quietly.

Daddy picked him up and hugged him. "Thanks, Son."

They all stood quietly in the doorway. "Do you like it, Mandy Bug?" Daddy asked.

"It's fine, Daddy," she said, even though she wasn't sure. Right now, she wished she was with Mommy.

"There's even room for Barney at this house," said Daddy.

Mandy wondered if Barney would be as confused about where he lived as she was now.

When they got home, Mommy was reading in the living room and Barney was with her. Eddie climbed on her lap and put his thumb in his mouth. Mandy sat on the arm of the chair, and Spencer lay on the floor near her feet.

"So what's your daddy's house like?" she asked.

"I get to have my own room," Spencer said. "And there's even room for Barney. Mrs. Twitmeyer and Priscilla can stay here. Daddy said we could even build a tree house in the back yard."

Mandy saw Mommy's jaw tighten. "It's a nice house, Mommy," she said. "But it doesn't have curtains. I like this house better."

That night, Mommy listened at Mandy's bedside while she prayed.

"God bless Mommy and Daddy and Spencer and Eddie and all our pets. Bless our two houses, too. Make us all happy again." Mandy looked at Mommy and saw her eyes fill with tears.

Mandy couldn't hold back her own tears anymore. She felt Mommy's arms around her as she cried.

"Oh, Mommy," she said. "I want to have our family together again!"

"I know, Honey. I know, but..." Mommy began to cry. For the first time, Mandy noticed how pale and tired Mommy looked.

Then Mandy put her arms around Mommy and cried even more.

They hugged and comforted each other for a long time until Mandy fell asleep in Mommy's arms.

"Eddie, what did you do?" Mommy's voice sounded surprised and angry. "I thought you didn't do this anymore!"

"I'm sorry, Mommy." Eddie was crying.

It was true. He hadn't wet the bed in a long time, though Mandy noticed that Eddie had changed lately. He sucked his thumb and had pulled out some old baby toys. He had even asked Mommy to give him his juice in his old baby bottle.

"Now I'm going to be late for work," Mommy complained.

Mommy changed Eddie's sheets while Mandy poured cold cereal for everyone. She was tired of making breakfast every morning. Mommy hadn't made waffles in weeks.

"All of my friends' mothers make their breakfasts," Mandy said to Priscilla. "But now Mommy has a job. I wish she would stay home like she used to." Priscilla rubbed against Mandy's leg. "Why can't Daddy come back?" Mandy asked her. "Why can't we all be happy like we were at the beach?"

"*Oh*, Spencer!" Mommy cried. "Mandy, come help me!"

Mandy followed Mommy's voice to the bathroom. Spencer had gotten sick all over the sink. Yecch!

"Help him clean this up, Mandy, please," said Mommy. "And help him get ready for school."

"I can't go to school!" yelled Spencer. "I hate school!"

Mandy knew how she was feeling herself, so she didn't wonder why he hated school these days. She also had overheard his teacher tell Mommy that he often fell asleep in class and that he was starting to bully the other kids. Mandy had seen Spencer sitting alone at recess, and she knew he was losing his friends. His teacher said it was likely he was missing Daddy.

"Come on, Spence," Mandy said tenderly. "I'll take care of you."

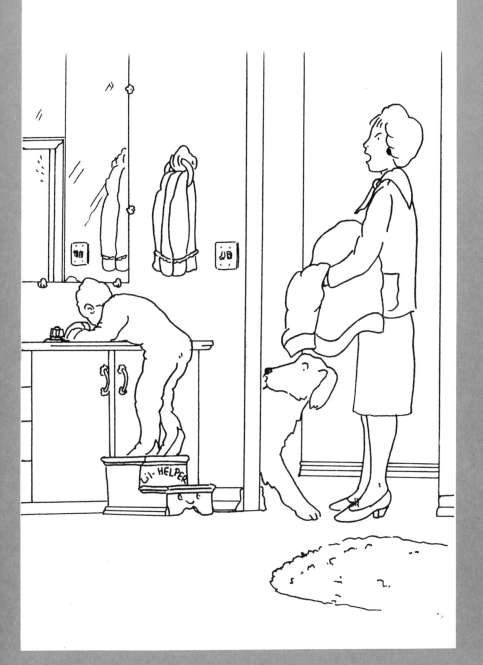

Mandy could see it all now. Daddy calls and asks Mommy for a date. They go out for a romantic dinner, and Daddy asks Mommy to marry him again. She says yes! They have a big wedding with the whole choir singing. Mandy is the flower girl...

"Mandy, I'm surprised at you." Mr. Esquivel interrupted her favorite daydream. "You seem to be having lots of trouble with your schoolwork. This spelling test just doesn't measure up."

Mandy hated to disappoint Mr. Esquivel, but right now she didn't care. Daddy was gone; that was all that mattered.

"What's troubling you, Mandy?" asked Mr. Esquivel. "Is everything okay at home?"

Didn't he know? Mandy thought the whole school knew, even though she hadn't told a soul except her best friends.

"My parents...my daddy...they're..." Mandy didn't know how to tell Mr. Esquivel. What would he think of her? She looked at the floor and twisted her braids with her fingers.

"My family is getting a divorce," she said. How she hated the sound of that word.

Mr. Esquivel knelt beside her and touched her arm. "I'm so sorry, Mandy," he said. "I know this is really hard on you."

Mandy loved Mr. Esquivel. But how could he know how she felt? Did he know how much she missed Daddy? Could he understand how hard it was with Mommy's new job?

Mr. Esquivel spoke softly, so only Mandy could hear.

"My parents divorced when I was a little older than you," he said. "It was really *awful*. My dad moved out, and I had to help Mom care for my younger sister."

Mandy wiped tears from her eyes. Would she ever feel happy again? She looked at Mr. Esquivel. He was smiling softly at her.

"I'd like you and your parents to see our school counselor, Mrs. Hendrix, as soon as possible, maybe even tomorrow. I know she'll be able to help. Would that be okay?"

Mandy looked at the floor. She wasn't sure about talking to a stranger. Still, Mr. Esquivel was her friend, and she trusted him. He really did understand what her family was going through. Finally, she looked up and slowly nodded her head. Mr. Esquivel smiled. Then he reached over and patted her hand.

"Things will get better, Mandy. I promise," he said as he stood up.

Mandy fidgeted as she waited on the chair outside Mrs. Hendrix's office. Mommy had come from work a while ago and was already inside. Daddy was late.

"Mandy," called Daddy from the doorway. "Sorry I'm late. Is your mom here?"

"She's talking to Mrs. Hendrix, Daddy," said Mandy. Daddy leaned over to hug Mandy and then knocked on the office door and went in.

Mandy counted the tiles on the office floor. She watched Mrs. Talbot, the secretary, type three letters and answer six phone calls. She twisted her braids and tied and untied the bow.

How long were Mrs. Hendrix and her parents going to talk? Did they forget she was out here?

Finally, the door opened, and Mrs. Hendrix poked her head out.

"Mandy, would you please come in now?"

Suddenly, she wished the time to wait would be longer. Slowly, Mandy stood up and walked into the office. Mrs. Hendrix was smiling, but Mommy and Daddy looked very serious. Mandy walked over and leaned against Mommy's leg as Mommy reached down and hugged her. Mrs. Hendrix sat in a chair near the desk. It was a pretty room with a big doll's house near the window and flowers on a table against the wall. The curtains had more flowers. Mommy and Daddy were both there, and suddenly, Mandy didn't feel so afraid.

Mandy got to talk about how she had been feeling since Daddy left. She told them how much she wished they could all be a family again and how lonely she felt when it was Friday but there was no Daddy coming home from a trip. She talked about the changes with Mommy's new job, how she hated going to the day care center after school, and how tired she was of fish sticks and cold cereal. Mommy and Daddy seemed surprised when she told them how all the kids hated having two houses even if Daddy's house was big and nice. She told them about a picture that Eddie had drawn of himself cut in half with half of himself in Mommy's house and the other half in Daddy's.

"I can never remember where my toys or clothes are, and I'm always afraid I'll leave my books or homework at the wrong house," Mandy told them. Mandy was speaking quite loudly, and her face felt hot. She didn't know why, but she felt angry. "And I don't like it when Daddy asks us all about what we do at Mommy's house or when Mommy wants all the details of what we did with Daddy," she said.

Mandy stopped suddenly and buried her face in Mommy's lap. Mommy stroked her hair. Mandy could hear Mrs. Hendrix's voice, but she didn't look up.

"Mandy, you certainly sound angry!" said the counselor. "I'm not surprised, with all the changes that have been happening in your life! Has anyone ever asked you what you preferred to happen?"

Slowly, Mandy raised her head and looked at Mrs. Hendrix. She checked to see if the counselor might be teasing her, but Mrs. Hendrix's face was serious, and her eyes were very kind.

The idea of anyone asking what she wanted was strange. Usually, nobody asked children about grown-up things! Why would Mrs. Hendrix even mention it? Mandy just looked at the counselor's kind face, but she didn't know what to say.

Finally, Daddy spoke. "Mandy, you know your mother and I were with Mrs. Hendrix for a while before you came in. One of the things she explained to us is that you and your brothers are very affected by any decisions Mommy and I make, and you should have a chance to tell us what you think. We might not be able to do what you prefer. But we can always listen and try to understand how you feel."

"I'm afraid," said Mommy, "that we haven't been very sensitive to you children. Mrs. Hendrix has pointed this out."

"Mandy," said Mrs. Hendrix, "even though your mommy and daddy are getting divorced, they are still your parents, and they will always be your family. Nothing can change that.

"But sometimes, when grown-ups are angry with each other, they forget that the children in the family can feel angry, too. Sometimes they even want to bring you into their fights and have you take sides.

"That's a bad idea. Your parents' problems belong to them, not to you or your brothers. You don't ever need to take sides or love one more than the other."

"Daddy and I don't ever want that to happen," said Mommy. "But sometimes, when Daddy and I are angry with each other, we forget that what we want for you is to know how much we both love you.

"Mandy, I hope you and the boys can forgive me someday for the things I've said and done that didn't help you. And I promise to try to be more sensitive to you when things are changing."

"Me, too," said Daddy. "Your mother and I don't seem to agree often these days. But this is one thing on which we agree completely. Mandy, I'm sorry for the times I've neglected you and the boys and not been there when you needed me. I was being selfish because I felt so terrible about the divorce. I intend to tell this to your brothers, too."

Mandy had never been so surprised. Her parents—apologizing to her! Daddy was looking straight at her, and Mommy was sobbing softly into a tissue.

Mrs. Hendrix spoke gently. "Mandy, after speaking with your parents, I know they love you and your brothers. But their pain about the end of their marriage has kept them from supporting you as well as they want to.

"Today, they are asking you to forgive them. They can't live together anymore. But they can be your family even though you have two houses. The problems of separate homes can be worked out. I can help you, and gradually, you'll all feel more comfortable.

"Mandy, getting a divorce is always difficult," Mrs. Hendrix said, "but when a family decides to cooperate with each other, it can be a lot better. We are talking to you first today because you are the oldest child. Are you willing to help?"

Mandy suddenly felt very grown up. She moved to the chair between Mommy and Daddy and sat with her legs crossed, like Mommy.

"What do I have to do?" Mandy asked.

"You have to tell your parents how you feel when you hurt, not keep it inside," said Mrs. Hendrix. "I'd like you to meet with me once in a while and let me know how things are going. And if you are having problems in class, you need to tell Mr. Esquivel. He wants to help you, too.

"Mandy, do you think you can do those things?" Mrs. Hendrix asked.

Mandy thought for a moment. "But sometimes I'm not sure how I feel, so how can I tell someone else?" she asked.

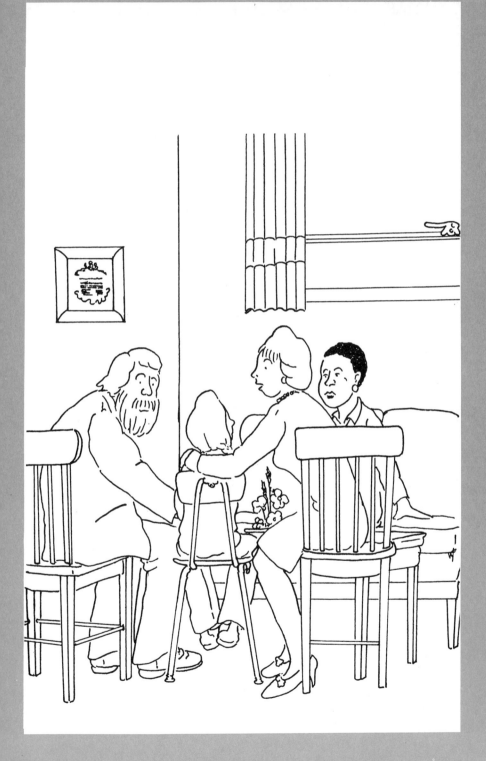

"That's a really good question," said the counselor. "If you know that you don't feel good about something, or if you are having a bad-feeling day, you can tell one of us or Mr. Esquivel, and we'll help you figure out what's really happening."

"Adults can have problems with feelings, too," Daddy said. "Some days I feel terrible, but I don't know why. So I just huff and puff all day, bothering other people with my bad mood."

Mandy giggled. She thought of the Big Bad Wolf, with Daddy's face, huffing and puffing at the Little Pigs' houses.

"That's when I need to stop and try to figure out what I'm upset about," he continued. "I may even need a counselor of my own to help me. Let's you and I agree to try to figure out our own feelings and to ask someone for help if we need that, okay?" Daddy looked deep into Mandy's eyes.

"But what if I'm with Daddy, but I'm mad at Mommy?" she asked Mrs. Hendrix. "I can't tell Daddy about that."

"I agree," said the counselor. "That might be awkward. But you could call me and talk to me, couldn't you? Even if I'm not at my office, I have a machine. You could leave a message, and I would call you back." Mrs. Hendrix leaned toward her and handed her a card with her name and phone number. Mandy felt more and more grown up.

"Yes, I could do that," she said. "But what about the boys? They're younger than I am, and they won't understand all this."

"We'll speak with your brothers," Daddy said. "Mrs. Hendrix has offered to help them as well. Mandy, I think we can work this through. It won't be easy. But if we persevere, we can do it—as sure as the bees squeeze their knees."

Mandy smiled. She loved Daddy so much.

It was three weeks later, and Mandy felt really scared.

"My Daddy's not here!" cried Mandy to Miss Kodama, the gym teacher. "He was supposed to pick me up today!"

Miss Kodama spoke softly and touched Mandy's shoulder. "Mandy, I'm sure he's coming. Just let me put away these balls, and I'll go outside and wait with you."

Mandy sat on a chair in the playground office and wiggled her foot nervously. Suddenly, Mommy and Mrs. Hendrix walked by the office door and saw her.

"Mandy, why are you in here?" asked Mommy. "I've been looking all over for you."

"Mommy," cried Mandy, running to her mother. "Daddy's not here!"

"But Mandy," said Mommy, "it's my turn today to pick you up." Mandy's eyes widened, and she burst into tears.

"Mommy," she cried, "I can't keep track of where I'm supposed to be every day. I try to remember, but I can't! Why can't our family be like we used to be?"

Mommy took Mandy into her arms, right there in the playground office. She spoke softly into Mandy's hair. "I know, Mandykins," she said. Mommy hadn't called her that in a long time. "I know how scary this all is. Some days, I wonder how we'll make it!

"But we will make it. I know we will. We have Mrs. Hendrix to help. We're all trying to work together. I just keep reminding myself of those things. In the end, I know we'll make it. But in the meantime, this is a very confusing and scary time."

Mandy pulled away a bit and looked into Mommy's eyes. "You mean, you get scared, too?" she asked.

"Oh, yes, Mandy, I certainly get scared, especially when I'm not sure about how things will work with all the changes. Almost every day, I have scary times." Mommy was chuckling a bit, and Mandy smiled back at her. Suddenly, she didn't feel quite so afraid.

Mrs. Hendrix spoke now. "Mandy, you and your mommy are going through a lot of the same things, only your experiences relate to your life as a child and hers are adult experiences. But both children and adults get confused and afraid when familiar things change."

This was a new idea for Mandy. Maybe that was why Mommy sometimes cried at night when the lights were out. Mandy could hear her from her own bedroom.

She looked at Mrs. Hendrix. "Do you think Daddy gets scared, too?"

Mrs. Hendrix smiled. "Oh, I'm sure he does," she said. "Everyone gets scared sometimes, and your daddy has had a great many changes and losses in his life lately."

Mandy looked back at Mommy. "But if you and Daddy are confused and scared, too, why don't you get married again? Then nothing would be scary anymore, and we could all be happy again."

Mommy stood up and led Mandy by the hand to the chair where Mandy had sat earlier. She sat down and Mandy leaned against her knees and looked into her face. Mommy looked like she was thinking.

Finally, Mommy spoke, "Mandy, if you think back to when Daddy and I were living together, you'll likely remember that we weren't at all happy. Do you remember the fights we used to have?" Mandy nodded. She didn't like to remember. She looked at the floor.

Mommy went on. "Clearly, Mandy, living together, being married, is not the best answer for us. For none of us. So we need to figure out how to live apart and still support you and your brothers as your parents. Being married again wouldn't solve the problems. For me, Mandy, the thought of getting back into that fighting is more scary than being divorced."

Mandy remembered the fights. She remembered the loud voices, the harsh words, the slamming doors. At least now, that didn't happen often. Her fights with Spencer and Eddie didn't feel the same as when Mommy and Daddy had fought.

"You know where your daddy lives, and you know where I live," Mommy continued. "Two homes can be confusing, I know. But, have you noticed, Mandy, that you actually see more of your daddy than you used to when we lived together?"

Mommy was right, Mandy thought. Daddy was hardly ever away now, and he called nearly every day. She and her brothers slept at his house at least two nights every week and sometimes went out for dinner in between.

"Shall we go home?" Mommy asked. "The boys are in the car, and I have a nice dinner ready."

"I'm sorry I got mixed up," she said to Mrs. Hendrix and Miss Kodama. "I caused a lot of problems for everybody."

"That's fine, Mandy," said Miss Kodama. "You let me know whenever I can help. I know this is a confusing time for you." Her smile was warm and friendly.

As Mandy walked away with Mommy, she thought about how many people really wanted to help. There were Mr. Esquivel, Mrs. Hendrix, Miss Kodama, and their friends at church.

Maybe, like Mommy said, they'd get through it, in the end.

To the Caregiver

The HELPING CHILDREN WHO HURT series is designed to assist adult caregivers with the difficult and often painful task of helping children understand their own feelings about tragedies they experience.

One of the hardest tasks of helping children lies in moving past our adult understandings of life and into the space of the child. We who care for children understand that they often do not perceive and interpret life events in the same ways as adults. But often, we do not know *how* their thinking process and feelings are operating. And, children being children, they usually are not able to explain their own experiences. So all the well-meant attention in the world can be wasted because we are not able to communicate.

These little books will help with that communication. They will stimulate discussion and encourage both adult and child to examine and share their own experiences. The hints in this section will give some useful insights to adult caregivers and will help you find direction for your conversations. There are no rules about how to use the books; our suggestions are meant only to serve as beginnings. For some, the presence of the questions will provide courage to begin to address areas which otherwise would have been full of mystery and fear. No more will parents need to say, "I know I need to speak with my child about _____, but I don't know how to speak with my child about _____." No more will teachers need to think, "Johnny must be upset about , but how do I reach out to him?" With the HELPING CHILDREN WHO HURT books, you will be able to make a start in helping both the child and yourself unravel the complicated grief situations of normal life.

The series is designed to respond especially to the needs and development of four- to eight-year olds. This is an age when children are perceiving life and reacting with many obvious behaviors but are usually not able to understand or explain their responses. Adults who care for and about them may ache for their pain but not know how to reach out and support.

Be a Caring Presence

The first thing to remember is that your presence is probably the most important factor. Constancy, fidelity—these are not just old-fashioned words. They are the base upon which any relationship with children must be built. If a child knows you can be depended upon, that you will be faithful in the relationship, he will then believe that he is important to you. And if the child believes that you really care, then he will begin to trust you, even with the scary experiences which are so hard to understand.

Don't expect that you can just turn up at a tough time and speak some words of wisdom which will help the child's pain and bond the two of you forever. Even the most competent therapist knows that these things take time. The child will need to interact with you—"feel you out"—and decide if you are reliable and trustworthy. One term to describe this reality is "investment." The child will check whether you are really invested in the relationship or if it is not very important to you.

The other mistake adults often make—once they know they need a "relationship" before the child will allow them to break into the painful areas—is to become a "smotherer." The thought process is something like this, "I want to help this child, so first I'll *prove* that I'm a friend."

Respect the Child's Boundaries

Children, like adults, have boundaries, but often, children are not as good as older people at defining those boundaries to others. They need to be respected. Always use the same respectful voice and stance with a child in pain as you would with an adult. If you want to touch the child, make sure your touch is wanted. If you are not sure, ask, "I'd really like a hug right now. Would that be okay with you?"

Listen!

The ideal, of course, is that you already have a relationship with the child who is hurting. Even then, you may not know how to talk about that specific area of life which is causing the pain. Take the book and sit in a quiet place together. Then tell the child, "I think what has been happening to your family is really awful. If I were you, I think I'd be pretty mixed up. Is that how you feel?" Then really listen. The child may not be as confused as you think, or she may share some of her confusion with you. When you have listened, affirm the questions and also the answers which the child has worked out. Those answers likely "fit" that child's life needs and must be respected.

At this point, tell the child that you have found a book about a family which experienced something like she is experiencing. Say that you'd like to read the book with her and that she can tell you if she thinks it is realistic. This sort of approach values the child's insights and encourages her to listen to the story.

Don't try to analyze the child's answers or give solutions. Most painful situations can't be "fixed"; they can only be survived. And children, like adults, usually find courage and strength to survive through compassionate support from another person. The most supportive message you can give a child is that whatever he is feeling, he has a friend who will try to understand. If he is angry or frustrated or terribly sad, tell him those feelings are normal, given what he is going through.

Allow the Child to Grieve

Often, adults think that children should always be happy. A grandparent dies, a puppy is killed by a car, Mommy and Dad separate, and adults tell the child that everything will be fine. We justify Granny's death by saying "Old people die, you know." We bring home a new puppy and expect the child to immediately love it. We say, "Don't worry. Mommy and Dad both still love you, so this won't hurt you or change your life."

In reality, childhood is no more a happy time than is adulthood. In fact, because children have much less control over circumstances and far fewer life experiences upon which they can reflect when crisis comes, these times are often more traumatic for them than for adults. Think back on your own childhood. Were you always happy? We (the authors) have never met a person who was. Children, like adults, are experiencing life, with all its ups and downs. We need to allow them their own feelings and to validate their journeys.

So be sure that, whatever the child expresses, you assure her that she is normal. You might want to share with her about something in your life which made you feel as she does today. That will establish her sense of your empathy; it will also help her know that she can get through this time because someone else has also felt this terrible and survived.

Watch for Signs of Guilt Feelings

One emotion (or perhaps it is a judgment) which children often feel in the midst of tragedy is guilt. Children perceive the world as revolving around themselves. So, if Mommy and Daddy separate, it must be because "I wasn't a good girl." Or maybe, "If I hadn't run through the house, Mommy wouldn't have become sick and our baby wouldn't have been born too soon."

This is really the only way a child can perceive things. It is very hard for them to understand that bad things just happen without being caused by any person.

Your job is to reassure the child that you understand why he feels that way while also telling him your perception of the situation—that Mommy and Daddy had a lot of fights and couldn't live together, and it had nothing to do with the child. Or that the baby got sick inside Mommy, and that would have happened even if he had played as quietly as a mouse.

Be aware that the child may have received "blaming" messages from important adults. Unfortunately, this often happens. Adults, frustrated and tired, say things like, "Now look what you've done!" and little people take them at their word. So it is often useful, if you perceive serious and strong guilt feelings in your child, to ask her why she thinks she might be to blame. Did she hear something which made her think that? Listen carefully; the child may give you good insight into how you can help.

These books are all designed to reflect the attitude that no child is responsible for tragedy. There is never a hint of that concept, and each book contains a solid explanation of why the tragedy did happen. If you think that guilt is a factor for your child, you might want to ask him if he thinks the child in the story is at fault, and that will help you either to understand his perspective or to compare his reality with that of the child in the story. Guilt feelings usually don't go away in one meeting, but eventually, with continued support and affirmation, they can be alleviated.

Fidelity, presence, a listening ear, respect, and a willingness to affirm—these are the best ways to help. Now, sit back and read the story. Let it touch you. Look at the questions only after reading the story. When you are with your child, don't use the questions like a school examination. Use them only to begin the conversation. For example, "How do you suppose Mandy might have felt when she heard her parents arguing?"

Each book in the series illustrates the family in the story calling upon their faith experience as a resource in a difficult time. There is no reason why this faith expression should be identical to that of the child you are helping. This aspect has been included in the stories for two reasons. To begin, very often, God is presented in unhelpful ways to people in pain. For example, "It was God's will that Grandma died." This sort of presentation does not allow people to freely experience all the emotions, including anger, which arise during normal grief. It is our hope that these stories will offer some helpful alternatives for those who want to help the child draw upon her faith experience. If the examples in the story are different from what would be meaningful for your child, feel free to say something like, "Isn't it interesting what this family believes? What do you (or 'your family' or 'our family') think about _____?" Second, children themselves, whether or not they have been introduced to faith concepts in their families, very often, especially in crisis times, have "God questions." The inclusion of some faith expression in the book opens doors for adult caregivers to invite the child to share his thoughts and questions and to process how those thoughts are impacting his responses to the crisis.

Enjoy this time with your special child; remember, friends who can speak about painful things grow closer together. We hope these books will be gifts for your relationship.

Notes about
OUR FAMILY IS DIVORCING

This book is about a family with three young children at various stages of development and their parents. Each person is impacted differently by the ending of the parents' marriage, but the effect on each touches the lives of the others. The children feel the effects of Mommy's grief. When Spencer vomits, it affects Mandy's life. When the children struggle to adjust to the reality of separate parental homes, Daddy and Mommy share their struggles. Nobody is alone when a family system changes.

But for the children most of all, there is a sense of loss of control over their lives. They are told that the parents will separate. They are told that they have rooms in both homes. They feel the impact of Mommy's new job and Daddy's absence. They are not consulted about any of these new realities.

It is important to realize that, for children, the *status quo* is their security. Children will invariably choose the familiar over the unknown. So life in a home where parents are constantly bickering, or even abusive, is preferable to alternative options. There are two reasons for this. One is that small children have not yet developed the ability to imagine something with which they are not familiar. The other reason for this preference is that small children have struggled all their lives to develop mastery and control over the familiar home environment. Even if that environment is not a healthy one, they will struggle to maintain what control they have because they are afraid that a changed environment may not work for them. Because of this fear, it is important to include even small children in as many decisions as possible, within the scope of their ability to understand. For example, in the story *Our Family Is Divorcing*, when Daddy moved into his new house, he might have shown all the bedrooms to the children, asking them to work out a sleeping arrangement. They might have chosen to all share one room or two might have chosen to sleep together. Or they might have chosen separate rooms but different ones than Daddy would have assigned. In this process, the children would have developed some sense of ownership over the house and seen it as part of life over which they had some control. It would then be important, of course, to allow the children to choose the furniture and decorating schemes for their spaces (within Daddy's budget) even if those were not to Daddy's taste.

Or even earlier, if it were possible, Daddy might have shown the children two suitable houses and asked the children to help him decide which he would rent.

This is an example of giving children some sense of empowerment in the changes to their lives.

Another important aspect is the absolute necessity to allow children to love both their parents without qualifications. In the story, Mommy was quite vocal about her angry feelings about Daddy. This was confusing for the children, who began to feel that they might have to choose between their parents. Children are not able to make these choices without emotional trauma. So, unless there is an abusive situation, it is vital that the children be encouraged to have ongoing relationships with both parents and that neither parent criticizes the other or tries to use the child as a go-between with the other.

It is the sense of a loss of control which often causes children, even those who have never been inside a church, to turn to prayer. They look for a powerful advocate who can make even grownups behave as they wish. The only one more powerful than grownups is God. Nearly every child of school age has heard about God, from other children or on television. Even if their parents do not believe in God, children do not have the ability to separate the real from the imaginary, and if they have heard about God, then God is real for them. So although the children in the story are taken to church, real-life children whose families have no religious rituals will often pray at times like this. You will notice that the prayers of these children have two things in common. They are ego-centric (they ask for outcomes which the children desire), and they appeal to a powerful figure who can make the grownups come into line. This is not selfishness but a natural response within the children's developmental stages. They are not capable of perceiving their world in any other way. Any grownup working with a child of this age will be more helpful if s/he can frame support within the ways the child thinks because the child cannot come around to the adult's way of thinking.

In divorce more than any other loss, we tend to neglect the pain of children. We presume that they will just keep on with their lives and not be affected by the major changes in the family structure. We think that they might even be happy for their parents because separation will improve the quality of lifestyle for the adults and lessen the tension in the home. But children are completely egocentric. They are not selfish, but they have not developed the ability to empathize with other people's emotional needs. In the story, Mandy is peripherally aware that Mommy seems happier after the separation, but she is unable to understand, for a long time, that this is a worthwhile end for the reality that she has had to give up Daddy's live-in presence. In the end, she may understand that things are not going to change. But until she translates what Mommy is saying into an understanding of the lessening of tension which affects her own life, she is unable to accept that Mommy's pain is enough reason to explain why Daddy had to move out.

Children, just like many adults, are comfortable with the familiar and do not like changes. That is why a child will enjoy hearing a story he has heard a hundred times before. The familiar words and pictures and rhythms will delight and give him a sense of mastery. And if his family usually eats mashed potatoes with fried chicken, he will be affronted if someone else prepares fried chicken and rice.

In a family separation, many familiar things change. There is no way to prevent this from happening. But one way to reassure a child is to point out what is still the same. Familiar routines should be maintained as much as possible. Bedtimes and meals and trips to the library should be carried out just as if the separation had not happened. This is often very difficult for parents who are distracted and struggling with their own painful realities. But for the sake of the children, it is very important. The main reason why Mandy panicked when Daddy was not at school to pick her up was that she was upset with all the changes and frightened by a loss of control over her life. In this case, it might have been helpful for the parents to sit with a teacher and the children and explain a chart which detailed who would pick them up each day. The chart could then be placed at a convenient spot in the classroom for the children to check when they felt insecure (much the same way as an adult will check a daily calendar to verify appointments). This would remove the children's sense of a hit-or-miss schedule and give them some sense of routine and control. It would also help them realize that their needs were important to their parents.

Because they are egocentric, children cannot understand that their parents' motivation for divorce does not include their own behavior. They often believe that if they had been better behaved their parents would have stayed together. And because they are often confused by their own feelings and unable to tell people how they feel, they will act out their confusion and hurt. In the story, Mandy copes by repeating to herself what Mommy and Daddy said about the separation not being the fault of the children. Although she does not understand it, she is able to cling to it. But she still covers all bases by trying to be nicer to her brothers and keeping up her grades. Her brothers, however, are not quite as old and experienced and are unable to cling to their parents' reassurances. Spencer, like many children, acts out his questions in aggressive, attention-getting behavior. Subconsciously, his motivation may be, "If I am naughty enough, both my parents will have to notice and will get together to teach me to behave." Or he may be thinking, "If I am a naughty enough boy that my Daddy had to leave, I guess I'd better act that way." Eddie, on the other hand, reverts to baby behavior. He may be thinking, "Daddy wanted to live here when I was little and cute. Maybe if I am like that again, he'll come back." Or he might just be longing for the nurturing and cuddling he received as a baby but not know how a big boy could claim the attention he needs.

There are professional people who can help children and their parents understand why they are acting as they are. If you care for a child who is unable to understand or articulate what she is feeling, encourage her parents to find someone who can help with this process.

It is very helpful for children to understand what their parents are feeling when the family separates. In the story, Daddy does not call for several days. One can only imagine what the children are thinking and wondering during this time. When he does come, he turns up looking like a stranger, pretends that everything is wonderful, and presents the new house. It would have been much better if he had waited a bit longer to grow his beard and had taken the children for dinner first and listened to their concerns and expressed his. Even better, he might have come to see them much sooner and called them often, filling them in on what was happening in his life. It is reassuring to a child to know that his parents are also struggling and trust him enough to share their concerns. (Note: This does not mean that either parent should share intimate details of his/her relationship with the other parent or with people s/he may be dating. This is grown-up material and will only confuse the child.) It encourages him, for his part, to share his fears and concerns. Like adults, children are helped by sharing their struggles with someone who cares and understands. If this is not happening and you are caregiver for a child living in this sort of turmoil, you can do a great favor to this little one by helping him share his confusion and fears. There may be no solutions to the family turmoil, but having someone to listen and help him understand how it is impacting him personally can be a great support for coping.

So now we invite you to use this book for yourself and a child you care about. Find a quiet place and read the story together. Let the child interrupt you, or stop yourself at appropriate places and ask open questions—the kind which don't have a *right or wrong* answer. You might preface your questions with, "I wonder..." or "Why do you suppose...?" The questions on the next page are only suggestions. This is not to be used as a "workbook" but as a resource. Any question which begins a train of thought and conversation is appropriate.

Questions for Discussion

1. What kind of family do you think this was when Daddy lived at home?

2. How do you think Mandy might have felt when she heard her parents arguing?

3. Why do you think Mommy and Daddy told the children it wasn't their fault that Daddy would be leaving?

4. Why do you think Daddy stayed away such a long time before he came to see the children? What do you think the children thought while Daddy was away?

5. How might the children have felt when they saw Daddy's beard and his new house?

6. Why do you think Spencer might be acting so strangely at school? Why would Eddie act like a baby?

7. How did Mandy feel when she spoke with her parents and Mrs. Hendrix? Was it okay that she felt angry part of the time?

8. Should we try to think of some ways this family could get used to having parents who live in two houses?

9. Who are some people who are helping you or your family get used to all the new things in your lives?

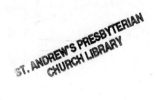